Turtle and Snake Go Camping

To all the great libraries and
librarians, and to the kids
who find their adventures there.

VIKING
Published by the Penguin Group
Penguin Putnam Books for Young Readers,
345 Hudson Street, New York, New York 10014, U.S.A.
Penguin Books Ltd, 27 Wrights Lane, London W8 5TZ, England
Penguin Books Australia Ltd, Ringwood, Victoria, Australia
Penguin Books Canada Ltd, 10 Alcorn Avenue, Toronto, Ontario, Canada M4V 3B2
Penguin Books (N.Z.) Ltd, 182-190 Wairau Road, Auckland 10, New Zealand

Penguin Books Ltd, Registered Offices: Harmondsworth, Middlesex, England

First published by Viking and Puffin Books,
divisions of Penguin Putnam Books for Young Readers, 2000

1 3 5 7 9 10 8 6 4 2

CIP data is available from the Library of Congress.

Viking ISBN 0-670-88866-4

Viking® and Easy-to-Read® are registered trademarks of Penguin Putnam Inc.

Printed in Hong Kong
Set in Bookman

Reading Level 1.4

Turtle and Snake Go Camping

by Kate Spohn

VIKING

Let's go camping!

Pack the tent.

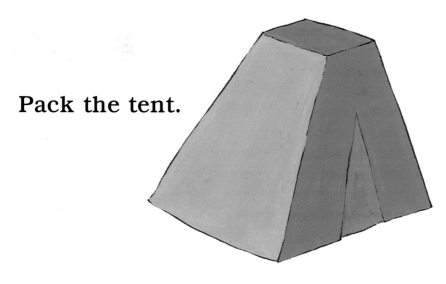

Pack the
sleeping bags.

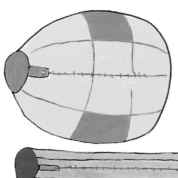

Pack the food.

March, march

around the trees.

in the brook.

Row, row across the pond.

There it is.
A perfect spot to camp.

Up goes the tent.

Down go the sleeping bags.

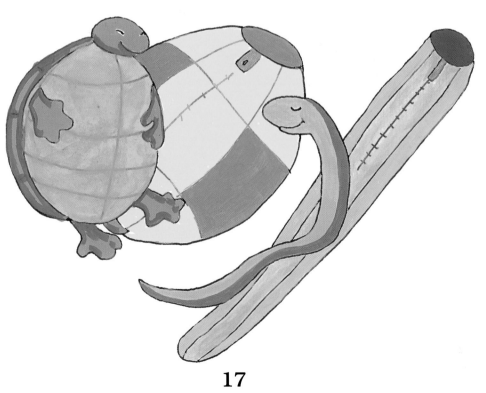

Out comes the food.

19

Row, row across the pond.

March, march around the trees.

There it is.
A perfect spot to camp.